To: Maisie
A magical story
for a magical you

From:

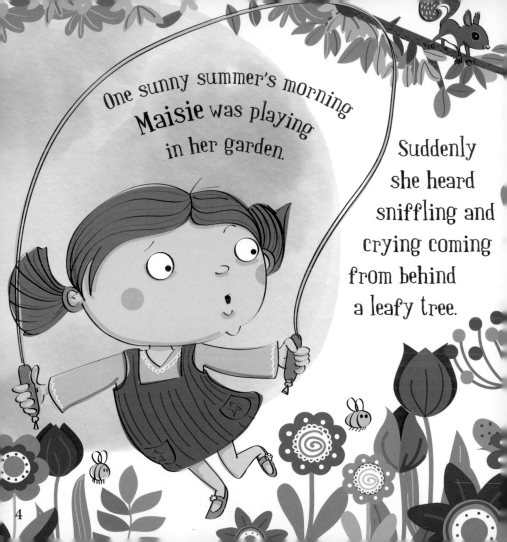

One sunny summer's morning **Maisie** was playing in her garden.

Suddenly she heard sniffling and crying coming from behind a leafy tree.

4

Maisie
tiptoed closer and closer
to the whimpering.

When she peeked around the tree
Maisie was shocked to see a
little white and purple, sad-looking...

5

"Hello, my name is **Maisie**,
what's your name and why are you
crying?" she asked the unicorn.

"I'm Sparkle, and I've lost all the magic colours on my rainbow horn from giving out **too many wishes**," said the unicorn.

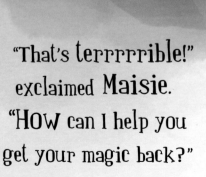

"That's terrrrrible!" exclaimed Maisie. "HOW can I help you get your magic back?"

8

"Well," said Sparkle, "as I become happier colour returns to my horn and when I have all seven CO OURS my magic powers are restored and I can give out wishes again."

Maisie had a think, and a wonder and a ponder...

...**what** could she do?

"**I've got it!**" shrieked Maisie.

"We need to do things that will bring back Sparkle's sparkle!"

10

#1

SO, they tried playing a game of hide-and-seek.

Sparkle wasn't very good at it but because she enjoyed the game so much the first rainbow colour returned to her horn - ruby RED!

ching!

11

#2

Then they sat on squishy bean bags drinking hot chocolate and eating rainbow-coloured marshmallows. This made **Sparkle** very happy!

slurrrp

With a slurrrp of her hot chocolate, brilliant ORANGE flashed up on her horn.

"I know what you need now," said **Maisie**...

"...a PAMPER day!"

So they wrapped up in fluffy robes, had their nails painted, and were so thoroughly **pampered** that sunny YELLOW

pinged back on to Sparkle's horn.

#3

13

#4

Next up on their fun-filled mission was bouncing UP and down

doing somersaults on Maisie's trampoline.

They were having so much fun that Sparkle' emerald GREEN band reappeared on her horn

#5

Hungry from so much bouncing, the two friends went inside to make unicorn shaped cupcakes.

14

There was flour and eggs everywhere when the colour sky BLUE appeared on Sparkle's horn.

There were only two more colours to go and Sparkle was feeling SO much happier, but what could they do to get the last two?

"AHA!" exclaimed **Maisie**, as she remembered the **fun fair** had just come to town!

#6

...whizzed round and round and on the last loop-the-loop Sparkle squeaked with s...

They zipped up and down,

16

...light...

...a bright **INDIGO** band appeared!

There was just **one** more colour to go.

Exhausted from all the fun the two friends settled down to a magical film and some popcorn. Sparkle was so happy that bold VIOLET, the very last rainbow colour, popped back on to her horn.

"That's it! Thank you Maisie!" laughed Sparkle. "You have made me so happy that **all** of my magical rainbow COLOURS have reappeared and I can grant wishes again."

"Now, what wish would YOU like?" asked Sparkle. "I wish, wish, wish I could see the Unicorn Kingdom," Maisie said hopefully.

19

With a
ZING and a ZAP,
a WHIZZ and a WHIRL,
Maisie and Sparkle soared up,
up, up through the
wondrous rainbow.
Then in a flash
of twinkling pink light...

Maisie couldn't **believe** her eyes,
she was **really** there and all because she
had helped a **unicorn** have **oodles** of **fun!**

The End

COLOUR
ME IN